Encoded Illusion

By

Kevin J. Crosby

Dedication

When I was in kindergarten, they asked me what I wanted to be when I grew up. Without hesitation, I said, "James Bond."

To everyone who helped me get there—this one's for you.

Even the smallest drop in the bucket makes a wave.

Acknowledgment

I cannot thank the U.S. Department of Defense and our allies enough for their protection, while brats like me stopped bad-guys growing up. Instructors who encouraged me to tutor bring back fond memories, as have everyone else who bolstered my experiences learning how things work, or why they don't.

My research wouldn't have been made possible without assistance from the Seattle Public Library et al granting me access to rare items like a collection of World War Two postage stamps and J. Edgar Hoover's ghostwritten book. Just as soon as I finished my research, they tore down the downtown branch and rebuilt it to resemble a crystal cathedral which makes me feel dizzy when I walk inside due to not having developed my "sea legs" yet.

Table of Contents

Greetings

We are living through a silent revolution—one not marked by marching armies or fiery speeches, but by the subtle reshaping of how we think, feel, and perceive reality itself. The battleground is not found in the streets or on digital screens alone, but in the most sacred terrain of all: the human mind.

This manuscript is not a call to reject science, progress, or innovation. Rather, it is a call to remember what it means to be fully, consciously human in a world increasingly designed to make us forget. Across education, technology, and our own latent capacities, a pattern emerges: systems that once promised liberation are now quietly redirecting our mental energy toward compliance, distraction, and dependency.

Chapter One explores how the very structure of modern society is designed to inhibit independent thought. From the early foundations of industrial-style education to the algorithmic manipulation of media and language, we are trained not to think critically, but to follow orders, memorize scripts, and remain perpetually entertained. This is not accidental. As the chapter shows, the "dumbing down" of the population is both systemic and strategic. A society that no longer questions, that accepts official narratives without reflection, is a society easily steered whether toward consumerism, complacency, or digital servitude.

But this erosion of mental sovereignty does not stop in the classroom or on the television screen. It seeps into the very fabric of our evolution.

Chapter Two brings us to the frontier of human-machine integration—a landscape where innovation walks hand in hand with manipulation. The cyborg era is no longer speculative. From brain implants to neural data harvesting, from emotion-modulating headsets to corporate access to mental telemetry, our thoughts are no longer private. What was once the realm of science fiction is being rapidly normalized as the next phase in human enhancement. But behind the marketing of performance upgrades lies a more disturbing truth: every device that connects our minds to the cloud opens a portal for control, surveillance, and programming.

The philosophical question raised is this: can we still claim autonomy when our very preferences, fears, and memories can be altered? If our mind becomes a programmable interface, then who holds the keyboard? Is the future one where we expand our humanity—or one where we lose the right to define it for ourselves?

Amid these revelations, **Chapter Three** reminds us of an older truth—one that may hold the key to reclaiming our mental sovereignty. It delves into extra-sensory perception (ESP) and the untapped potential of the human mind. Here, the narrative shifts from defense to rediscovery. What if the mind can do more than process external stimuli? What if it can reach across distances, perceive hidden knowledge, or affect reality in subtle but profound ways? Though mainstream science may scoff, declassified military research and recurring patterns in collective consciousness studies suggest something far more powerful at play.

From ancient spiritual traditions to modern neuroscience, the evidence points toward a forgotten truth: the mind is not just a product of biology—it is a tool, perhaps even a gateway. Intuition, remote viewing, and the ability to influence physical systems through focused intent are not just metaphysical curiosities. They are symptoms of a capacity that has been suppressed, ridiculed, or left unexplored—not because they lack merit, but because their existence threatens the control mechanisms of society.

Together, these three chapters present a unified message: our minds are under siege, but they are also more powerful than we've been led to believe.

This book does not offer easy answers or miracle fixes. What it offers is a lens —a way to see what has been hidden in plain sight. It invites the reader to question not only the narratives fed to them but the very structures that shape those narratives. It asks: Who benefits when we stop thinking for ourselves? Who gains when we doubt our instincts? And what would change if we remembered the full scope of what we're capable of?

The stakes are immense. The technologies we embrace today will shape the consciousness of tomorrow. The educational systems we tolerate today will define how future generations perceive their worth, their identity, and their agency—the quiet force that drives them to make their own choices. And the spiritual, intuitive, and psychological faculties we choose to explore—or ignore—will determine whether we remain programmable tools or reclaimers of our own destiny.

The future isn't simply digital, synthetic, or algorithmic. The future is contested. Between the lines of code and the waves of distraction, a choice still remains. Will we surrender to the architecture of manipulation? Or will we awaken to our inherent intelligence, our forgotten senses, and our immeasurable capacity for self-realization?

What lies ahead is not just a technological crossroads, but a human one.

This is the starting point.

Chapter One

We enter this world with a profound sense of curiosity. From the very first breath, we reach outward, touch unfamiliar objects, taste new sensations, and marvel at the world around us. Yet, somewhere along life's path, that innate curiosity is gradually dulled. The vibrant impulse to question and explore is slowly replaced by rigid structures, standardized processes, and predetermined answers. What begins as gentle guidance, in the hands of certain systems, transforms into a method of control. Make no mistake: a quiet war is being waged against independent thought.

This battle is not fought with guns or missiles but with far more subtle weapons. It is conducted quietly—in classrooms, on television screens, through our devices, and even within the language we use. It is subtle, persistent, and unyielding—a deliberate reduction of intellectual capacity and a conditioning of minds to prefer simplicity over complexity, distraction over discovery, compliance over curiosity.

In the modern education system, evidence of this phenomenon is everywhere. Rather than cultivating the boundless energy of creativity and critical thinking, schools frequently funnel students into narrow, inflexible molds. The emphasis rests on examination results, standardized curricula, and conformity. Children are instructed to memorize facts for assessments, to follow directions without deviation, and to remain seated in orderly rows while their natural creativity quietly withers. The questions that truly matter—"Why is this so?", "Who benefits from this rule?", "What information remains hidden from us?"—are neither encouraged nor rewarded. Instead, students are guided toward careers and lifestyles that value efficiency over discernment and insight.

In fact, the structure of public education in the United States was modeled not on intellectual expansion, but industrial compliance. The Prussian model—which emphasized obedience, punctuality, and standardized instruction— became the framework adopted by the U.S. after 1900. John Taylor Gatto, an outspoken critic and award-winning teacher, famously called public schools "training centers for subordination." This wasn't accidental. As the *Skews.Me* article outlines, major figures in early education reform, including Horace Mann and Edward Thorndike, believed education should serve to "fit children for the role predetermined by their social class."

These ideas were reinforced by influential elites like Edward Bernays—the "father of public relations" and nephew of Sigmund Freud. Bernays believed that the average citizen was incapable of intelligent decision-making and needed to be led by a small, enlightened elite. In his 1928 book *Propaganda,* he argued that "manipulating public opinion" was not just acceptable—it was necessary to preserve order. That logic didn't stay in advertising; it leaked directly into how societies educated, entertained, and informed their citizens.

By the time they leave these institutions, most students have been conditioned to trust authority, accept information at face value, and suppress their instinct to challenge accepted truths. Those who dare to think differently are often dismissed as troublemakers, eccentrics, or outsiders. Yet, ironically, it is precisely these unconventional thinkers who the world most desperately needs.

However, the classroom is only the beginning. The media seamlessly continues where formal education ends, offering a steady stream of distraction and superficiality. The contemporary media landscape is saturated with celebrity scandals, manufactured outrage, and mindless entertainment. Significant issues are reduced to oversimplified soundbites, stripped of nuance, and delivered with emotional bait designed to provoke rather than to inform. The constant repetition of slogans, talking points, and outrage cycles leaves little room for reflection or comprehension.

The effect is deliberate. As the *Skews.Me* article notes, the so-called "dumbing down" isn't just poor content—it's precision-targeted simplification. In the 1950s, bestselling novels had an average reading level equivalent to the twelfth grade. Today's popular fiction sits around the seventh-grade level—not because readers got younger, but because attention spans and expectations were shaped to settle for less.

The cumulative consequence is widespread mental exhaustion as frustration leads to aggression. People are inundated with information yet starved for understanding. The ceaseless flood of headlines, notifications, and sensational stories shortens attention spans and fosters impatience with complexity. The subtle truths that reside within ambiguity and nuance become uncomfortable. Individuals gravitate toward overly simplistic narratives—good or evil, right or wrong, and even black or white. The world is seldom so simple, but grasping its complexity requires effort—an effort society increasingly discourages.

Even language has been corroded. Our ancestors understood the power of words and used them with great care, knowing that language shapes thought. Same was the case with hieroglyphics; they weren't just primitive doodles but sophisticated scriptures designed to bridge the gap between the abstract and the literal, similar to the emojis that we use today but with more nuance. Though in the modern age, communication has been reduced to fragments: tweets, text messages, emojis, and memes.

Each technological advancement in communication has made it easier to connect, but has come at a cost. We exchange depth for speed, clarity for brevity. Vocabulary shrinks, sentences fragment, and with that, the ability to express—and thus to think—in nuanced ways diminishes. This deterioration is not merely cosmetic; it is existential. When one cannot articulate complex ideas, one struggles to conceive them. Thought becomes confined by the limitations of language.

George Orwell articulated this peril with chilling clarity in *1984*, written in 1949. He warned that the control of language equates to the control of thought—by limiting the words available, one limits the range of ideas that can exist. Today, this form of control is more insidious and no less threatening. It is embedded in social media algorithms that reward short, incendiary content over thoughtful discourse. It is found in the carefully crafted language of corporate public relations, designed to obscure rather than illuminate. It thrives in entertainment that distracts instead of enlightening.

IQ test manipulation is another quiet front in this war. As outlined in the *Skews.Me* article, average IQ scores have been artificially pegged at 100 through a process called "test norming." In this system, every few years, new IQ tests are recalibrated so that the average result still reads as 100—even if actual performance has declined. This has masked a long-term downward trend in analytical thinking skills, especially in younger generations.

According to the U.S. Department of Education, only 12% of high school seniors are proficient in

U.S. history. And that's not due to lack of effort—it's the outcome of a system designed to suppress context, reduce timelines, and avoid controversial content. In other words, a society that doesn't know where it came from is easier to mislead about where it's going.

This slow erosion of independent thought is not merely a cultural trend but a deliberate instrument of power. A populace that cannot think critically is far easier to manipulate. A society distracted by trivial amusements and divided by orchestrated outrage is unlikely to notice the gradual erosion of its freedoms. Those who dare to question prevailing narratives are easily marginalized, their voices drowned out in a sea of noise and distraction.

However, every technological enhancement carries a profound cost. When our thoughts are transmitted through devices, who truly owns them? This isn't just a hypothetical question—real-world examples are already emerging. Take the Emotiv EEG headset, for instance. Buried in its Terms of Use is a clause about data ownership that raises an unsettling reality: the electrical impulses of the human mind, once considered the last bastion of privacy, can now be recorded, stored, and potentially monetized. If our thoughts can be captured, who decides how they're used?

And what happens when memory itself can be altered or enhanced? Who holds the power to shape the narrative of our own minds? The tools that promise to expand human potential also open the door to unprecedented control. The surveillance of yesterday relied on cameras and informants. The surveillance of tomorrow may live inside us, embedded in neural implants and cognitive monitoring systems—not watching from a distance, but operating from within.

Meanwhile, schools increasingly resemble behavioral correctional centers more than places of learning. Between 1999 and 2018, more than 200,000 children were arrested in schools across the U.S., often for nonviolent behavior. In one infamous case from Albuquerque, New Mexico, a 13-year-old was handcuffed and booked for burping in class. This is not discipline; it's criminalization. The *Skews.Me* article compares this to a prison pipeline, complete with uniforms, surveillance cameras, lockdown drills, and an overriding focus on obedience.

These questions aren't for some distant future. They are here now, pressing and urgent. Decades ago, the 1983 film *Brainstorm* imagined a world where human consciousness could be recorded and shared, inspiring a generation of thinkers and researchers. I was among them, drawn to the study of the brain as early as 1988. Yet, despite the early fascination, it wasn't until 2013 that institutions began releasing their own research on brain-to-brain interfaces. What was once science fiction is now taking shape, faster than we ever expected.

The war on intelligence is not just waged against the intellect—it targets spirit, imagination, and internal power. As the *Skews.Me* article hints, there's a broader agenda at work: to suppress any form of consciousness that might awaken an individual to their own agency. That includes intuition, spirituality, and the latent powers of human perception often relegated to pseudoscience. What is not measurable is made mockable. What cannot be monetized is made marginal.

This is not just about controlling information—it's about colonizing consciousness. Consider the DARPA-funded study in which a 16-wire electrode array was implanted in rats. One group was trained in a task, the second was not. Yet after transferring the recorded neural signals, the untrained rats could perform the task instantly. As Dr. Geoff Ling said at a DARPA event, "For this rat, we reduced the learning period from eight weeks down to seconds."

If learning can be uploaded, who decides what gets downloaded? What if knowledge becomes a commodity controlled by the highest bidder or the most powerful regime? The promise of progress could quickly become the machinery of mental uniformity.

The conditioning of society—through educational systems, media manipulation, and technological seduction—may not solely be about maintaining external control. It may also serve to prevent the awakening of deeper human potential. The most threatening individual to any system of control is not merely one who questions authority, but one who places unwavering trust in their own mind and spirit over externally imposed narratives.

There exists a profound possibility—both unsettling and exhilarating—that we are capable of far more than we have ever been permitted to believe. The human mind is not a static instrument but an evolving force, capable of remarkable perception and insight when freed from imposed limitations.

The central question then becomes whether we will surrender our cognitive sovereignty to external programming or reclaim it. Will we accept distraction, conformity, and artificial augmentation as the zenith of progress, or will we turn inward, cultivating the lost arts of deep thinking, courageous questioning, and instinctive trust?

This quiet war on human intelligence has been waged for generations. Its tools are subtle yet devastating: the dulling of curiosity, the erosion of language, the suppression of questioning, and the seductive allure of convenience. Yet the antidote remains within each of us—awareness, critical thinking, self-trust, and the audacity to ask the forbidden questions.

The struggle for humanity's future is not taking place on distant battlefields, nor solely in corporate boardrooms or technological laboratories. It is unfolding within each mind, in each thought, and in every decision to question or conform, to seek understanding or passively accept.

In the chapters to come, we will explore the hidden structures that sustain this war—the systems, technologies, and psychological manipulations shaping contemporary society.

We will examine the promises and dangers of cyborg technology, the enigma of untapped human potential, and the ancient wisdom that may still hold the keys to liberation.

But before we can look ahead, we must first recognize where we stand. We are poised on a precipice, gazing out over a world both dazzling in promise and disquieting in its trajectory. The path forward is ours to choose. Will we remain passive passengers in a future driven by machines, or will we reclaim the power of thought, imagination, and authentic intelligence?

The choice has never been more pressing. And it begins with awakening.

Chapter Two

The human body is an extraordinary construct—an intricate network of cells, nerves, and impulses that has developed and refined itself over millennia. Our senses link us to the external world; our minds interpret that world, and our hearts respond to it with emotion and instinct. For the vast majority of human history, we have regarded our biological makeup as both a gift and a limitation. It shaped the rhythms of life and grounded our sense of reality.

Yet now, poised on the brink of a new technological era, the distinctions between biology and machinery are beginning to dissolve. Medical science, computing, and engineering have converged to produce tools that do not merely assist human functions but merge with them. We are no longer passive users of technology; we are becoming integrated with it. Devices that once sat outside our bodies now communicate directly with our neural systems. This shift has altered the trajectory of human evolution, introducing a form of self-directed adaptation that bypasses natural selection.

Encoded Illusion

No longer is the human body the sole domain of organic processes. With every microchip, implant, and neural link, we redefine what it means to be alive. Whether through wearable technology that monitors our physiology or implants that enhance cognition, we are gradually transforming into cyborgs—part human, part machine, and increasingly dependent on our synthetic extensions.

This transformation is neither distant nor speculative; it is unfolding before us, subtly yet profoundly. When we first embraced the use of pacemakers to regulate our heartbeats and cochlear implants to restore hearing, we initiated the convergence of human biology and advanced technology. Today, prosthetic limbs that respond to neural impulses, retinal implants that restore sight, and brain-computer interfaces that enable thoughts to control external devices are not the imaginings of science fiction, but r eal and present advancements. These remarkable developments, born of human ingenuity in medicine and engineering, have already redefined what it means to be human.

And it is not just the physically impaired who benefit. Enhancement technologies are increasingly marketed to healthy individuals under the premise of maximizing potential—think faster reflexes, improved memory, deeper focus. What was once developed to compensate for loss is now sold as an upgrade, turning medical innovation into lifestyle optimization. This commodification of enhancement places the human body on a new economic frontier, where access and performance may soon define not only our health, but our worth.

At first glance, these technological achievements appear wholly beneficial. They restore lost abilities, enhance quality of life, and extend the scope of human capability. Yet beneath this sense of wonder lies an uncomfortable question that few are prepared to ask: what price do we pay for such advancements? Each technological enhancement integrated into the human body becomes a node—a point of connection to vast and complex technological networks. Anything connected, by its very nature, is vulnerable to access, surveillance, or manipulation.

Consider the course of this progression. In early laboratory experiments, monkeys learned to control robotic arms with mere thought. Paralyzed and locked-in patients with amyotrophic lateral sclerosis (ALS) have been granted the ability to communicate through neural implants. These breakthroughs are undoubtedly cause for celebration, marking milestones of progress. However, they represent merely the opening chapter of a longer narrative. The same technology that allows the brain to communicate with machines could, conceivably, facilitate communication in the opposite direction. The possibility of external influence—the transmission of information into the brain, rather than merely extracting data from it—is no longer theoretical; it is a genuine and pressing concern.

Put simply, the interface between human and machine is not a one-way conduit. That fact should give us pause. The rise of brain-to-device communication brings with it the real threat of network-to-brain manipulation. If our thoughts can direct machines, it follows that machines—and those who control them—might soon influence our thoughts. This would not be control through persuasion or suggestion, but through direct neural stimulation. It would mean bypassing language, reason, and even awareness.

Envision a scenario in which the thoughts you believe to be your own are shaped by external forces. Picture memories susceptible to alteration, emotions artificially induced or suppressed with a digital command. Such notions are no longer confined to speculative fiction. Researchers are already experimenting with methods to implant false memories and modulate emotional states by stimulating specific regions of the brain. What begins as a therapeutic intervention for trauma or mood disorders could, if unchecked, become a mechanism for subtle and pervasive mind control.

These possibilities raise profound questions about agency, urgency, and the means to make effective change. What is free will in a world where our mental landscape can be hacked? Can we claim to be autonomous if our preferences, fears, and desires can be modified without our consent or even awareness? The erosion of these boundaries forces a reevaluation of what it means to be human in a digitally infused age.

The philosophical implications of these developments cannot be ignored. What becomes of the concept of self when elements of cognition are entrusted to algorithms? When decisions are no longer informed by instinct, wisdom, or experience, but are instead influenced by computational processes operating invisibly within neural interfaces? The freedom to think and feel—once considered inviolable—could be reduced to programmable variables within a broader digital system.

Our dependency on external devices has already become deeply entrenched. Smartphones, for example, function as extensions of ourselves, serving as memory repositories, communication platforms, and navigational tools. We consult them incessantly for answers to questions that, in earlier times, we might have pondered independently while lost. While this dependence remains voluntary—for the moment—the migration of these devices from our hands and pockets into our bodies and eventually into our minds will cause the boundary between convenience and necessity to vanish.

The promises associated with these advancements will be enticing. We will be assured of faster learning, improved memory retention, and accelerated decision-making. Yet hidden beneath these promises lies a sobering reality: technology does not serve without conditions. Each neural implant and integrated device will come with dependencies—software updates, security protocols, and corporate oversight. The body will become hardware, the mind wetware, and both will be susceptible to remote management and interference.

The interest of governments and corporate entities in these technologies is already substantial. The U.S. Department of Defense, through DARPA, has heavily invested in brain-computer interface research, seeking to enhance soldier performance, reduce reaction times, and enable silent communication on the battlefield. While the military benefits are apparent, the civilian implications are deeply concerning. The same technologies designed for strategic advantage could be turned inward, enabling population control, the suppression of dissent, and the large-scale shaping of societal behavior.

Surveillance will no longer be confined to devices or digital footprints. It will extend into the most intimate aspects of human existence—our thoughts. Privacy, already fragile in the digital age, will become a relic of the past. There is no intrusion more profound than that which penetrates the sanctity of the human mind.

Yet beyond concerns of surveillance lies an even deeper fear: the erosion of the human spirit. Our imperfections—our doubts, struggles, and failures—are not merely hindrances but essential aspects of the human condition. Creativity often emerges from adversity, and resilience is born of repeated trials and errors. In a world where flaws are corrected by code and emotions are algorithmically balanced, will we lose the drive that inspires art, philosophy, and authentic human connection? Or will we drive education to teach us what needs to be taught?

We must also consider the profound societal consequences of these developments. Access to cognitive enhancements will not be equitable. Those with means will become faster, more intelligent, and more capable, widening the chasm between the enhanced and those who choose to remain organic. This stratification will extend beyond social or economic status into the biological realm, creating a new dimension of inequality that could shape the future of humanity in troubling ways.

Voices calling for caution do exist—ethicists, philosophers, and concerned citizens urging reflection and restraint. But they are often drowned out by the fervor of technological progress and the insatiable pursuit of profit. The companies driving these innovations are governed by competition and market incentives, not by philosophical contemplation. The central question is no longer whether these advancements are feasible, but whether they should be pursued without restraint.

The transformation, though still incomplete, is accelerating. The trajectory is unmistakable. The next phase will not involve wearable devices or minor implants but full neural integration—a seamless interface between the brain and cloud-based systems. Companies such as Neuralink are at the forefront of this effort, aiming to normalize implantable brain interfaces under the banner of cognitive enhancement. What was once science fiction is now marketed as the next stage in evolution.

But this "upgrade" carries implications that go beyond performance. The more intimate the link between the mind and the machine, the more vulnerable we become to cybernetic intrusions. Brainwave-reading headsets already exist commercially, promising relaxation tracking, sleep improvement, and even video game control. Yet, studies show they can also inadvertently expose private information—PIN numbers, emotional responses, and even political preferences. This isn't just about control—it's about entropy. Not thermodynamic, but cognitive. Every seamless upgrade subtly erodes our sense of self, leaving a hollow space, where identity once grew.

As the technology becomes more normalized, the social costs of opting out will increase. If education, employment, or healthcare start integrating neuro-enhanced expectations, the right to remain analog may quietly vanish. Children raised in these systems may grow up without meaningful agency, nudged by algorithms and monitored through implants, groomed for obedience rather than nurtured for individuality.

There remains another path—one that does not reject innovation but reclaims it through ethical vigilance and democratic control. This means prioritizing transparency in development, limiting exploitative patents, enforcing strict data protections, and ensuring that neural technologies serve human dignity—not undermine it.

The cyborg age is not inherently dystopian. It can alleviate suffering, empower those with disabilities, and amplify what is best in us. But without critical oversight and a shared moral compass, it may also become a quiet slide into digital authoritarianism. In a future where machines can read—or rewrite—the human mind, we must ask: what does it mean to be human? And are we prepared to defend that meaning?

We now stand on the precipice of a transformation as profound as the discovery of fire or the invention of written language. But we must ask ourselves with utmost sincerity: will we command the machine, or will the machine come to command us? The future may indeed be hybrid—but it must remain, above all else, resolutely human.

Chapter Three

Before the age of silicon processors, neural implants, algorithms, and vast digital networks, humankind faced a different frontier: the uncharted domain of the human social mind. Long before our understanding of circuitry and artificial intelligence, we pondered not only how the physical world functioned but whether reality itself could be influenced by deliberate thought. We spoke of instinct, intuition, and the immense potential of the unconscious mind. Across countless ancient civilizations, stories of remarkable mental faculties—telepathy, precognition, remote viewing—were passed down through sacred texts, folklore, and oral tradition.

In the modern world, such notions are frequently dismissed as mere fantasy or pseudoscience. Today's society, fixated on measurable results and rigid empirical proof, exhibits little tolerance for what cannot be easily quantified. Yet beneath that dismissal lingers an unsettling question: what if humanity has abandoned something genuine? What if human capability reaches far beyond the boundaries of neurons firing within the brain, extending into realms science has yet to grasp?

The concept of extra-sensory perception (ESP) still provokes skepticism in academic and professional circles, yet it remains one of the most intriguing and unexplored dimensions of consciousness. Despite widespread ridicule, powerful institutions—from military organizations to the private sector—have quietly devoted considerable resources to investigating these phenomena. The U.S. government's now-declassified Stargate Project, which spanned more than two decades, is one such example, where remote viewing and other psychic abilities were studied under rigorous and secretive conditions. The question naturally arises: why would substantial funds be allocated toward research into something thought to be illusory?

What they uncovered, though often obscured by secrecy or public denial, suggested possibilities far beyond traditional scientific understanding. Within controlled environments, participants described distant locations they had never seen, identified hidden objects, and made predictions that defied mere probability. While these results were inconsistent and not robust enough to dictate critical military decisions, they were nonetheless significant enough to leave scientists and intelligence agencies reluctant to dismiss the phenomena entirely.

If such abilities do, in fact, exist—even if only partially—they point to the possibility that the human mind is not confined to the brain-case that houses it. Consciousness may transcend the physical body, interacting with the world in ways yet to be explained, though if this premise holds, then thought itself could wield influence over reality far beyond what modern education and conventional science have taught us to believe.

Additional evidence comes from the natural world. Certain animals exhibit sensory capabilities that defy our conventional understanding. The platypus, for instance, can locate prey underwater using electrolocation—a biological form of electromagnetic perception enabled by thousands of electroreceptors on its bill. This allows the platypus to hunt effectively even with its eyes, ears, and nostrils closed. With an almost uncanny precision, it can detect electric fields as faint as 20 microvolts per centimeter—which is like detecting something as small as a grain of salt in a bathtub—tapping into this subtle energy like a sixth sense to navigate and interpret its surroundings.

Such biological examples suggest that perception may not be limited to sight, sound, smell, touch, and taste. Human beings, too, may possess dormant or underdeveloped perceptual abilities—sensory extensions that have been suppressed or overlooked by modern conditioning. Some researchers argue that humans may retain vestigial forms of magnetoreception, or the ability to detect magnetic fields. Studies have indicated that people might subconsciously orient themselves according to the Earth's magnetic field, a trait more pronounced in some species but potentially present in us as well.

The very definition of a "sense" has grown more complex. Scientists today recognize at least nine senses, with some arguing for as many as twenty-one. These include balance (equilibrioception), temperature sensing (thermoception), proprioception (body awareness), and pain detection (nociception). If we accept this expanded model, then why not also include intuition or mental perception— faculties that operate without clear physiological mechanisms but yield real, experiential data?

Encoded Illusion

In this context, ESP appears not as a wild anomaly but as part of a larger spectrum of perception that remains largely unmapped. Just as early scientists lacked the tools to detect bacteria, bat signals, or radiation at first, we may currently lack the instruments to properly measure the subtleties of consciousness and its potential reach.

But why, if there is even a kernel of truth to ESP, does mainstream society reject it so vehemently? The answer, perhaps, lies in the nature of authority and control. A society in which individuals trust their innate mental faculties— where people can perceive beyond official narratives and know without being instructed— is inherently more difficult to manipulate. If human beings realized their minds could tap into knowledge beyond sanctioned institutions, the entire apparatus of media manipulation and top-down control would begin to collapse.

It is more convenient for those in power to assert that knowledge is the domain of accredited experts and official channels. Any deviation from this paradigm is ridiculed as superstition or foolishness. The consequence is a cultural conditioning that teaches us to second-guess our instincts, suppress our intuitive understanding, and disregard the subtle, quiet signals of the subconscious mind.

Yet throughout history, the greatest innovators and visionaries have often credited inspiration that defied rational explanation. Nikola Tesla spoke of receiving fully formed ideas through vivid mental imagery. Albert Einstein's revolutionary concepts began with imaginative thought experiments and dreams that transcended conventional formulas. Artists, writers, and inventors frequently describe moments of sudden clarity that seem to arrive from beyond conscious reasoning.

Such moments may be more than mere flashes of creativity. They could represent glimpses of a deeper connection, a reminder that human consciousness is not isolated but part of a larger web. Ancient spiritual traditions around the world have long taught this principle. Indigenous shamans, Buddhist monks, and mystics across continents developed disciplines to quiet the analytical mind and access higher wisdom. Through meditation, fasting, rhythmic movement, and sensory deprivation, they entered altered states of consciousness that modern research suggests are conducive to enhanced intuitive abilities.

Encoded Illusion

Contemporary neuroscience has confirmed that altered states of consciousness correlate with measurable shifts in brain activity. In states of deep meditation or trance, brain waves transition from the fast-paced beta frequencies associated with everyday thought to slower alpha and theta frequencies, linked to creativity, intuition, and deeper cognitive processing. In these states, individuals frequently report experiences that resemble visions, telepathic exchanges, and moments of profound insight.

However, modern science, bound by its strict adherence to materialism and the necessity of reproducibility, finds it difficult to reconcile these findings with its current models. In the prevailing scientific view, consciousness is merely a byproduct of electrochemical interactions within the brain—no more than the sum of its biological processes. Accepting the possibility that consciousness might extend beyond the body challenges the very foundations of this worldview and raises unsettling questions about the nature of reality itself. Is the universe truly objective, or does the act of observation—the presence of consciousness—help shape it?

Quantum physics has already hinted that reality is not as fixed and unchanging as once believed. Subatomic particles behave differently when observed. Entangled particles appear to communicate instantly across vast distances, violating classical understandings of space and time. Could human consciousness be participating in these quantum mysteries? Certain researchers, such as Dean Radin and Rupert Sheldrake, have posited that it might.

Their controversial experiments have produced results that, while often met with skepticism, are statistically significant. Studies have suggested that human intention can influence random systems, and that knowledge can sometimes be perceived through means that defy ordinary explanation. Global networks of random number generators have shown anomalies during major world events, indicating that collective human focus might affect physical systems in subtle but detectable ways.

If these observations contain any truth, the implications are immense. It would suggest that reality is not merely something we observe but something we help to create. It would mean that the narratives of helplessness, dependency, and limitation imposed on us are not just disempowering stories, but deliberate fabrications meant to keep humanity subdued.

As technology advances, seeking to augment human potential through artificial means, perhaps the greater challenge lies in reclaiming the natural abilities we already possess. Why should we implant chips to enhance memory or cognition if the mind, through disciplined practice, can achieve remarkable feats on its own? Why should we rely on electronic devices to foster connection when we may already be connected through channels that transcend the physical realm?

Unlocking such potential, however, is neither simple nor instantaneous. It demands focus, commitment, and an unwavering willingness to cultivate self-trust. This path is not paved with technological shortcuts or instant solutions but with the slow, deliberate process of turning inward. It calls for reducing the distractions of modern life, confronting personal fears and doubts, and attuning oneself to the subtle, persistent voice within.

That inner voice, so often dismissed amid the chaos of daily existence, may be the key to human evolution. Intuition is not an archaic superstition but an advanced, highly evolved faculty. The subconscious mind processes vast amounts of information beyond our conscious capacity, detecting patterns, energies, and signals we cannot articulate. Yet, we are taught to silence this capacity in favor of external authority. But what if our intuition is, in fact, our most reliable guide?

There is also the profound matter of collective consciousness. If individual minds can influence reality, then what could be achieved through shared intention? Numerous experiments in focused group meditation and collective visualization have demonstrated tangible effects: reductions in crime rates, enhanced growth in plants, and changes in random number sequences. While critics often dismiss these results as anomalies, the recurrence of these patterns across multiple studies suggests otherwise. Where collective human focus is applied, real-world shifts occur.

Perhaps this is why modern society is saturated with noise, conflict, and distraction. A focused, unified human consciousness may be the most powerful force on the planet. Imagine a society not fragmented by fear or superficial division, but aligned in purpose—using focused thought to heal, to create, and to elevate. Such power would threaten those who seek control, yet it could liberate those who seek genuine progress and freedom.

This is not a new idea. In Matthew 19:30–20:16, Jesus told a parable about workers in a vineyard, answering the question of what heaven truly is. It wasn't described as a mystical realm to be passively inherited, but as something that must be cultivated—built. The laborers were called to work, each receiving their due not by seniority but by willingness. It's a teaching many institutions choose to ignore because it demands action rather than submission. And action—especially guided by unified, conscious intention—is exactly what threatens the foundations of control.

Ultimately, the question is not whether ESP exists but whether we, as a species, are willing to explore the full extent of our mental potential, or whether we will continue to surrender that exploration to machines. Will we outsource intuition to artificial intelligence, rely on algorithms for insight, and allow devices to mediate our connections? Or will we reclaim the ancient knowledge that human consciousness is far more expansive than we have been taught to believe?

The way forward is available to those who choose to seek it. It requires questioning established paradigms, embracing disciplined practice, and balancing skepticism with openness. Meditation, visualization, and focused mental discipline are not mere spiritual indulgences; they are tools for mastering the most powerful force we possess: our own consciousness.

This is not escapism or fantasy. It is the next logical frontier for human development. As society races toward ever more advanced technological augmentation, perhaps the most radical act of rebellion is to turn inward—to cultivate the abilities that have been with us all along. The future of humanity may not reside in silicon and circuits, but in the limitless power of the human mind and spirit.

We are not simply biological machines or digital avatars. We are thought, awareness, and will. If we choose to remember and nurture that truth, there are no boundaries to what we may ultimately achieve.

Final Word

The story told in these chapters is not one of despair, but of decision. It is not merely a warning, but a wake-up call—not to retreat from progress, but to meet it with awareness, clarity, and purpose.

We began with the quiet war on intelligence, tracing how education and media have gradually reshaped the human mind. A society that once revered curiosity and questioned deeply has been conditioned to memorize, obey, and scroll endlessly. This wasn't the accidental byproduct of modernization—it was engineered. Systems once meant to enlighten now function to contain. Thought itself has become something to be managed, packaged, and sold. The cost? A diminished capacity to understand the world on one's own terms.

From there, chapter two explores the murky waters of technological evolution confronting the emerging reality of human-machine integration — not as fantasy, but as current fact. Neural interfaces, cognitive enhancement devices, and direct brain-to-network connections are no longer experiments confined to research labs. They are being patented, marketed, and adopted. The implications are profound: not just for how we learn or heal, but for how we exist. Once your thoughts can be read, modified, or overwritten, freedom is no longer defined by law or borders—it is defined by code, and controlled by whoever writes it.

And yet, beyond these concerns lies a powerful revelation. The third chapter reminded us that the mind is not just a processor of information, but a vast, often misunderstood domain with capabilities we've barely begun to explore. Ancient cultures knew it. Modern science is beginning to suspect it. Human consciousness may possess faculties that transcend the five senses and challenge the materialist models of reality. The suppression of these potentials — intuition, ESP, collective consciousness—is not accidental either. A population that can feel deeply, perceive subtly, and connect directly is infinitely harder to manipulate.

Together, these chapters paint a picture of a pivotal moment in human history. On one side stands the promise of progress: faster learning, enhanced abilities, and new forms of intelligence. On the other, the risk of profound manipulation: programmable memory, artificial emotions, and an irreversible dependence on digital systems. In between is the human being—you, me, all of us—still capable of choosing which path to walk.

And that is the message this manuscript ultimately delivers: **we still have a choice.**

We can choose to remain passive, allowing our thoughts to be shaped by curated feeds, predictive algorithms, and synthetic enhancements—or we can choose to reclaim the right to think for ourselves. To steer the mind before it is steered for us. That means questioning what we're taught, thinking beyond what we're shown, and reconnecting with parts of ourselves we've been told are imaginary or unscientific. It means turning inward, not out of retreat, but as an act of radical reclamation.

Reclaiming the mind is not a rejection of technology or science. It's the opposite. It's demanding that these tools serve human dignity, rather than define it. It's recognizing that progress without philosophy becomes propaganda. Innovation without reflection becomes invasion.

This isn't an abstract idea—it's a daily practice. It starts in the choices we make every day:

☒ Do we engage with information critically, or consume it passively?

☒ Do we allow devices to think for us, or do we carve out time to think without them?

☒ Do we speak and write with care, or allow our language—and thus our thoughts—to be diminished by digital shorthand?

☒ Do we trust our instincts, or wait for external validation?

And finally, do we believe in our own potential—not the kind sold by tech companies, but the kind that emerges from silence, focus, and introspection?

We live in an age where everything is being quantified, tracked, and optimized. But the most meaningful parts of life—awe, insight, love, intuition—resist measurement. They are what make us human. They are what make us whole. And they are what's at stake. Between empathy and entropy, the future balances on a precarious limb dangling tantalizing treats. One reconnects us; the other reduces us. The battle is not just technical—it's emotional, even spiritual.

If we lose the ability to think freely, to feel deeply, and to connect authentically—not through apps but through empathy—we lose something far greater than privacy or even freedom. We lose the very essence of what it means to be alive.

But we haven't lost it yet.

This work is a challenge and an invitation. A challenge to resist the subtle colonization of consciousness. An invitation to rediscover the inner technologies we've carried all along: wonder, reflection, imagination, intuition, will.

The systems described in these pages are powerful, but they are not inevitable. They depend on our complicity, our fatigue, our belief that there is no other way. The moment we stop accepting that premise, everything begins to shift.

A better future will not be built solely through smarter machines or sharper code. It will be built by sharper minds—minds that remember who they are, what they're capable of, and why they matter.

As Jesus said in the parable of the vineyard (Matthew 19:30–20:16), heaven is not inherited— it is built. We are the laborers. And the time to begin the work is now.

So let this be the beginning—not just of new knowledge, but of a new awareness, though we must work together in harmony to make eternity a beautiful symphony rather than a raucous cacophony of unpleasant noise.

The mind is the last frontier—not just to explore, but to defend. A space no longer mapped by wonder, but increasingly mined by code. And now, more than ever, it is worth defending.

References

- Bernays, E. L. (1928). *Propaganda*. Horace Liveright.
- Defense Advanced Research Projects Agency (DARPA). *Brain-Computer Interface Research*.
- Gatto, J. T. (2005). *Dumbing Us Down: The Hidden Curriculum of Compulsory Schooling*. New Society Publishers.
- May, E. C., & Marwaha, S. B. (2018). *ESP Wars: East & West*. Crossroad Press.
- Orwell, G. (1949). *1984*. Secker & Warburg.
- Radin, D. (2006). *Entangled Minds: Extrasensory Experiences in a Quantum Reality*. New York: Paraview Pocket Books.
- Sheldrake, R. (2012). *The Science Delusion: Freeing the Spirit of Enquiry*. London: Coronet.

- Skews.Me, *Cyborgs*:

  https://skewsme.com/cyborgs.html

- Skews.Me, *Dumbing Down*:

  https://skewsme.com/dumbing-down.html

- Skews.Me, *ESP*:

  https://skewsme.com/esp.html

- The Holy Bible, New International Version. (1978). Zondervan.

- U.S. Department of Education. *National Assessment of Educational Progress (NAEP) Report on U.S. History Proficiency.*